CW00571613

Relaxing Bedtime Stories for Children

Best Collection Of Beautiful Adventures, Funny Dragons And Enchanted Creatures, Unicorns & More To Help Your Children To Fall Asleep Fast And With Smile

Written By

Margaret Milne

Table of Contents

DAMIEN AND MAX

The sun had begun to set and the room was slowly darkening but Damien

hadn't turned on the lights. His toys were scattered around the room, with

clothes strewn on every surface. 'Damien please stop playing video games'

Damien's mother called out to him but he ignored her. Continuing to play his

game, he felt the slightest satisfaction as he leveled up.

'Damien!' his mother said annoyed as she reached his bedroom to find him still

playing. Turning on the lights, she looked around the dirty room and sighed. 'I

told you to clean up an hour ago' she said as she began to pick up the dirty

clothes, clearing the floor. 'Can you please leave the room and go outside to play' his mother pleaded. Sighing, Damien grabbed his crutch and began to limp on one leg, his other bound in a cast.

It had only been a week but it felt like forever ago that he had fallen from the swings, fracturing his leg. He only managed to reach the living room when his healthy leg began to hurt. Sighing, he sat on the sofa and carefully placed his broken left leg on the table and massaged his right leg wondering why it had begun to hurt as well.

'DAMIEN' HIS MOTHER SIGHED AT STILL FINDING HIM INSIDE. 'MOM! IT HURTS' DAMIEN SAID HARSHLY AS HIS MOTHER RUSHED TO THE SIDE. 'WHAT? WH Zavier's Good Deeds

'Mom!' 'Moooooomm!' Zavier yelled excitedly, entering his house.

'In here dear!' his mother called from the kitchen. Zavier ran through the living room where his younger brother sat playing with his toys. He found his mother, sitting on the dining table with her laptop in front of her and her phone to her ear.

'Look at my new clothes' he said excitedly. Smiling, she said goodbye on the phone and spread her arms for Zavier to jump into. 'Oh my little boy! What did you get?' she asked smiling widely at her son's excitement.

'The Eid festival is just ten days away. Dad and I got new clothes' he said as his younger brother Danny crawled up to them. Overturning the bags in haste, he began to show his mother the new clothes he had gotten. He pulled out his blue shirt with white buttons and a white collar. He then showed the matching pants he had gotten, blue with little white boats on them. As he went through his shopping, his father walked in.

9

'Who's excited about Eid?' he asked and both his sons jumped in delight, their younger sister bobbing up and down in her crib. 'Now kids' their father said seriously sitting on the table. 'Eid isn't just about new clothes. It's about taking care of everyone around you' their father explained. 'Yep!' their mother joined in. 'Everyday! I want you to look around and see how you can help the people' their mother said. 'If you add a little goodness in the world, you will be surprised at how it finds a way back to you' she said and Zavier nodded a little absent mindedly, his attention focused on the clothes.

The next day, Zavier walked back home with his friends Alex and Mike. 'You know how my ball had been missing for a week?' Mike asked and Zavier and Beth nodded having listened to Mike complain all week long. 'So yesterday I opened the garden door and there was my ball' he told them excitedly.' My mum said it had been there all along' Mike said as Alex and Beth swung their bags to and fro listening to him. 'I don't believe it was there. I just think it missed me and found its way back to me' Mike concluded causing Beth to giggle. 'Things don't find their way back just like that. I still haven't found my bat that I lost last Christmas' she said and Zavier remembered his conversation with his mother.

'I don't know about the ball' he said laughing with Beth. 'But my mum says if you put something good out in the world, it finds a way back to you' he said. 'Well! I did help my neighbor find his dog last week. Maybe this was the goodness finding its way back' Mike said excitedly and the children wondered of the good things they could do.

Waving goodbye to his friends, Zavier went down his street and wondered how long it would take for his good deeds to come back to him. Sitting at the dinner table with his parents, he told them of his discussion with his friends. '-and so I'm wondering when my good deeds will come back to me' Zavier said causing his mother to laugh.

'Honey!' she said patiently. 'Do you plan to do good deeds so you will be rewarded and find things for yourself?' she asked and Zavier thought about it. 'I-' he began a little unsure. 'I don't think so but I'm not sure' he said and his mother sighed gently.

'Why do we do something nice for someone?' she asked causing him to think. 'To make them happy and because we can' he said and his mother nodded. 'Keep that in mind every time you get a chance to do something nice' his mother said. 'But what does putting goodness in the world mean?' he asked and she smiled. 'You will see' she said simply.

The next day Zavier was walking down the road when he saw an old man struggling with his shopping bags. 'Hello Mr. Martin' he waved at the old man. Running up to him, he took a few bags from him. 'You really shouldn't lift so much weight at your age' Zavier said causing Mr. Martin to laugh. 'Oh dear boy! Thank you for the help' he said as Zavier began to walk next to him. They walked the next block exchanging stories. 'You are a fine boy' Mr. Martin said as he put his bags down and took the ones from Zavier. 'Now I won't be as tired and I'll be able to go for a walk with my wife which makes her very happy' he told Zavier. Mrs. Martin had the kindest smile and Zavier smiled just thinking about it.

Returning from school, Beth, Mike and Zavier decided to stop at the park to play basketball. 'Whoever scores five baskets wins' Zavier exclaimed as they ran to the court. Beth and Mike stood on his sides as he threw the ball in the air. The three jumped for the ball and Beth being the tallest, got to it first. Dribbling it, she ran and jumped-

'SCOREEEE!' she yelled laughing. Before long the three ran breathlessly around for the ball, their laughter ringing around the court. 'I'm winning' Beth exclaimed as they breaked for water. Running to the side, Mike saw a little boy playing with the ball by himself. The boy would throw the ball, run after it, look at Mike and his friends and then throw the ball again. Catching Mike looking at him, he hurriedly moved to the side scared.

'He's alone' Mike said walking to Zavier and Beth. 'We could ask him to play with us' he said. 'You do need help so I don't beat you' Beth said laughing. As the three began to walk towards the boy, he stopped throwing his ball. Standing rooted to the ground, Mike was surprised to see the fear on his face. 'I wasn't doing anything' the boy said quickly hiding his ball behind him, as they neared him. Zavier frowned at his reaction. Barely two years younger and a head shorter then Zavier, the little boy had long black hair that covered his hair. 'Uh-' Mike began a little hesitant at the boy's reaction. 'We saw you playing by yourself and wondered if you wanted to play with us?' Beth said and the boy peered from behind his hair, his eyes widening.

'That is if you want to' Zavier said, smiling a little. 'I- I'd like that' the boy said a little hesitantly.

'I'm Jack' he said shyly. 'Zavier. Beth. Mike' Mike introduced them. They

walked to the court and he followed the three. They waited as he took off his

jacket, taking extra care to cover his ball with it. Splitting into teams of four,

they began to play. 'You are so bad' Beth laughed as she and Jack beat Mike

and Zavier. They took a break for water. Lost in conversation they didn't notice

Jack as he went to his jacket. 'Would you like to play with my ball?' he asked

shyly holding it forward.

'Wowww!' the three exclaimed. 'Ours is so torn and old' they complained

bouncing Zavier's ball around. 'Thanks man!' Beth said and Jack smiled. 'It's

brand new. Some boys took my old one when I was playing by myself' he told

them and Mike and Zavier exchanged looks. So that was why Jack had been

scared of them.

'You are our friend. You don't have to worry now' Beth reassured him and Jack

smiled brightly. Returning to the game, they laughed and chatted as Zavier and

Mike lost by a mile.

Days passed and the three friends made sure to put some goodness in the

world. Mike helped a girl find her puppy. Beth helped her old neighbor remove

the washing as it began to rain and Zavier made sure that no kid played by himself in the park. By the end of the week, the group of three friends had increased by eight and what a sight it was to see children of all ages playing together. It was a day before Eid and the children were playing in the park. The adults watched happily as the children played together, helping one another and looking out for each other.

'Go long!' Jack called out to Zavier.

Zavier kept walking back, his eyes focused on the ball in Jack's hand ready to catch it.

'Catch!' Jack said and Zavier jumped.

OW!

He cried out as his foot landed on a lose rock, twisting his ankle.

'Ow!' he cried as his friends rushed forward.

'Oh dear' Alexa said, one of their new friends who was much older than them.

'We should get him home' Mrs. Martin said, having walked slowly to the scene with Mr. Martin.

'Ow!' Zavier cried out, holding on to his leg as pain throbbed. Gently, his friends helped him to his good leg. They linked their arms around Zavier and then around one another.

'We're a human ambulance' Jenny, the youngest in the group said causing everyone to laugh, including Zavier. And just like that, linked with one another they moved through the streets in a formation, carrying Zavier.

'Someone! Ring the bell!' Beth panted under the crushing weight of her friend. The whole formation turned so the corner person could ring the bell causing them all to laugh louder. 'Ow!!! Hahaha! Oww!' Zavier continued to laugh and cry.

'What on earth-' his mother said as she opened the door to see eleven children standing shoulder to shoulder, with her son in the middle. Finally, breaking the formation, they handed Zavier to his father who carried him to the living room couch. 'What is it? What is it?' Questions bombarded him from all directions causing him to smile.

'Zavier seems to have a minor sprain' he said as bandaged him up. Settling in the couch and still laughing from the jokes that had been cracked constantly, Zavier bid goodye to his friends.

Telling his mother all about the incident, Zavier settled his head back ready to sleep. Just then his eyes fell on the freshly ironed clothes his mother had laid out for tomorrow. 'I won't be able to take any part in Eid celebrations' he said, his face falling. Every Eid he would go see his relatives and play with their children. It was a day of joy as everyone laughed and ate sweet things and now he would be missing it.

'We'll do something at home' his mother comforted him, giving him a kiss on his forehead. The next day Zavier woke up at the crack of dawn and prayed with his mother, not being able to go with his father. As he sat in his new clothes sadly watching the television, the doorbell rang.

'Hello!' Jack entered, wearing freshly ironed clothes his hair brushed neatly away from his face. 'I know it's Eid and you couldn't go to your relatives so my mom made this strawberry cheesecake for you' he said shyly, holding up the cake. 'Happy Eid' he smiled causing Zavier to smile. Just as Jack sat down, the bell rung again. 'Hello Mrs. Kahn!' Beth greeted Zavier's mother. 'Hey you!' she said to Zavier entering. Zavier was surprised to see she had dressed up as well. 'I know you couldn't travel today so mother sent this carrot cake' she said putting the cake next to Jack's. And like that one by one all his friends came to his house bearing sweets and wearing their finest clothes to celebrate Eid with him.

'This sure is one lovely Eid' Zavier's mother said seeing all of Zavier's friends playing together. Just as she was about to settle down the bell rung again. 'Now who might that be' she asked and they looked at each other confused. All of Zavier's friends were already here.

'Hello dears' Mr. and Mrs. Martin entered holding a box full of fudge. 'Zavier makes everyone so happy so we just couldn't bear to think of him sitting alone' Mr. Martin said. 'Happy Eid' Mrs. Martin smiled causing everyone to smile. Surrounded by his friends and family, Zavier felt his heart glow with happiness and understood how goodness found a way back.

ere? Did you damage the cast?' she asked immediately concerned but he pointed to the healthy leg he was massaging. Placing it in her lap, she massaged it until the pain disappeared.

'Do you want help?' his mother asked, pointing towards the door. Knowing how much his mother worried about him, Damien finally nodded. Helping him up, she carried most of the weight as they moved past the living room, out in the garden. Taking the gravel path, Damien inhaled deeply, being out after

18

forever. Settling on the lone bench in their garden, Damien rested his head on his mother's shoulder. 'The sun looks beautiful' he said surprising his mother as she looked up. With the Sun setting, the sky looked like it was lit by a red fire, its flames rising and spreading above the horizon-. 'You are beautiful' she said to her Sun, seeing his round childish features lit orange as the sun turned his brown curly hair to a darker shade. 'You're silly' Damien laughed at his mother and she smiled at the wonderful noise.

They sat in silence enjoying the evening when a car rolled in the driveway. 'Dad's here' Damien said attempting to get up but his mother placed a hand on his shoulder. 'Wait here' she said and he watched curiously as his father got out of the car with a box in his hands. 'What's that?' he asked but his mother simply smiled. 'Hi dad!' Damien called out as his father reached them, hugging him. 'Your father and I thought you would like some company in the house until your leg gets better' his mother said and Damien watched in amazement as the box wiggled in his father's hands. Putting it on the ground, he gently turned it to a side.

WOOF!

A gentle bark escaped from the box and Damien smiled. Hurriedly, moving forward he opened the flaps. Two round eyes stared up at him.

WOOF!

The little puppy barked again. Excitedly, Damien lifted the tiny creature out of the box. With light brown fur and tiny dark tail, the puppy struggled in Damien's hands trying to lick his face.

WOOF!

It barked again but Damien put him on the ground.

'Is this some joke?' he asked angrily. Back on the ground, the puppy limped, it's back leg missing.

'What? No!' his parents protested as Damien angrily got up. Ignoring the pain in his leg, he limped through the lawn even as his parents called him back. He reached his room and settled in front of the play station, deciding to never leave his room again. Before he could even turn his game on, his parents entered the room. 'Damien!' his father said sitting next to him. 'Do you think my leg will never heal?' Damien asked his voice thick with tears. Was he going to be like that puppy? 'No son! It's only a fracture. You heard the doctor. You will be back on our feet in no time' he said but Damien continued to cry. 'Then why did you get me a puppy with one missing leg?' he asked, wiping his eyes.

'Nobody wanted to adopt him at the shelter but I thought my son understands how difficult it can be to have an injured leg so I brought the little guy home' his father explained as Damien hiccupped. 'I didn't think anyone else could care more for the dog than you' he said and Damien finally wiped his eyes. 'You wanted me to help the little guy?' Damien asked and his father nodded. 'Have you seen those puppy eyes? Imagine him stuck all alone in a cage' his father said and Damien looked at him horrified. 'That little guy was in a cage?' he asked and his father nodded. 'Are you ready to meet him now?' his father asked as Damien wiped his face. Nodding, Damien grabbed his crutch and limped out to the living room.

WOOF!

The little puppy barked, running up to Damien. 'Careful' Damien laughed as it licked his toe, tickling his feet. 'What's his name?' he asked his father, lifting the tiny creature in his hands. 'His name is Max' his father said. Damien stared into those kind round eyes and scratched him behind the ears. 'Max' he said gently as the puppy barked trying to lick Damien's face.

His parents went about putting dinner together but Damien couldn't keep his eyes away from his puppy. He watched in amusement as Max went around the room sniffing everything. 'Here Maxi Max!' Damien called as Max sniffed the flowers lying on the table, climbing on its edge with his front two legs.

'Careful Max!' Damien called out.

The next moment several things happened at once. The table toppled with Max's weight bringing the flower vase down with a crash. Damien in an attempt to protect Max had leapt off the sofa forgetting his hurt leg.

OW!

He cried out as he landed on his injured leg. 'My leg!' Damien cried out. His parents rushed to the room at the noise. 'My leg!' Damien cried as pain shot through his leg. 'Woof!' Max barked trying to climb onto Damien's lap but Damien pushed him away. 'Get away you silly dog' he cried in pain. His parents lifted him in his arms, carrying him to the hospital. Returning late at night after constant reassurances from the doctor that nothing had been damaged, Damien dosed off in the car. Finding himself being carried to bed, he stirred gently as he felt a tiny warm weight settle next to him on the bed. Damien woke up the next morning and found the tiny warm space next to him empty.

Wondering if he had imagined the warm weight, he got up only to find his leg still hurting.

WOOF!

Max barked as Damien left his room to go the bathroom. Ignoring the puppy, Damien went to the bathroom. After brushing his teeth, he opened the door to find Max still waiting for him. 'Go away' he grumbled, making his way back to his room ready to play video games. Max followed him inside. As Damien settled on his sofa, Max followed him. Running around his ankles in circles, Max barked wanting to play. Annoyed, Max lifted his legs from the floor.

Woof!

Max barked gently, as he tried to climb the sofa. 'Get out!' Damien said harshly. 'Out!' he repeated pointing to his door. Damien felt a pang of guilt as Max's ears drooped. With sad eyes, Max walked out of the room settling just outside Damien's door. The week passed with Damien playing his video games, bound in his room with Max waiting just outside his door. Anytime Damien got up, Max would raise his head excitedly only to lie back down in disappointment when Damien ignored him.

One afternoon, Damien sat on his bed having returned from a doctor's visit. Angry at not getting the cast off just yet, he lay back on the bed. Looking outside he saw his mother outside with Max. Ignoring them, he turned on his playstation and began to play. As a game ended, he looked up to see his mother talking to the neighbor Mrs. Cathy as Max tried to catch birds. He watched as his mother went inside Mrs. Catchy's house. Ignoring them, he returned to his game.

'What is this thing?' he heard someone call from outside.

WOOF!

Hearing Max bark ,Damien looked up. Something about the bark sounded off. He saw a group of boys from his class surrounding Max as the puppy tried to get away.

'Where's your leg?' a boy Damien knew as David asked, prodding Max while his friends laughed. Max struggled to get away from the boys but anytime he tried to escape, they gently nudged him back in the circle with their feet. Angry, Damien lifted his crutches and rushed outside, speeding up at Max's distressed barks.

'Just what are you doing?' Damien asked the boys angrily.

'Oh hey Damien!' David said looking up. Max began to bark even louder at seeing Damien. 'We were just messing with this thing' he said as the boys laughed.

'With my puppy?' Damien asked raising his eyebrows. Sensing the distraction Max wobbled to Damien, hiding behind him.

'Oh! We-uh- we didn't know he was yours' David said, embarrassed. 'We just thought he was funny without his legs' he continued, rubbing his neck.

'You think I'm funny with my broken leg?' Damien asked getting angry both at himself and these boys.

'No. No. Of course not!' the boy next to David said.

'If you don't think me getting hurt is funny, then why would bother such a helpless creature?' Damien asked and the boys lowered their heads in shame. 'We didn't think' David admitted looking apologetically at Max. Turning on their heels, they walked away. Damien limped to the bench and settled there as Max followed. Angry at himself as well, Damien gently lifted the puppy. Seeing the boys bully Max made him realise how badly he had treated his puppy for his own mistake. 'I'm so silly. I can't take care of myself and I took it out on you Maxi Max!' Damien said sadly.

Woof!

Max barked. 'I am silly aren't I? Look how big I am compared to you and I still can't take care of myself' Damien said smiling at his puppy as he tried to lick Damien's face. 'You really are a good boy' Damien said, holding Max close to his heart vowing to never be mean again.

That night as he got ready for bed, he found Max lying outside his door. Getting in bed, Damien lifted his blanket. 'Get in here you' he said as Max barked happily, running to the bed. Struggling to climb the bed, he finally made it and settled next to Damien. Feeling the familiar weight of warmth, Damien looked at his puppy accusingly. 'You have been sneaking in my bed after I fall asleep, haven't you' he asked

Woof?

Max barked innocently as his eyes lit up with mischief.

The day before Damien's cast was to come off, he sat with his parents in the living room. 'You sign here' he instructed his parents pointing to his cast. Just as they finished signing, a crash sounded from the kitchen. 'Oh boy!' Damien's mother said as Max emerged from the kitchen, his face covered with ketchup. 'Oh Max!' Damien laughed as his puppy ran up to him. Booping him gently on the cast, Max barked proudly. As he moved away they all laughed. There on top of the cast was a big red mark!

'Now everyone has signed my cast' Damien exclaimed causing everyone to laugh.

FERRIER'S ADVENTURE

Elfie beeped his horn loudly. 'Move it Ferier' he called out waking Ferier up.

Ferier opened his eyes to see his old uncle Elfie standing in front of him. He

was an old red truck with faded paint that was peeling in places. With scratches

on every surface and bumper stickers older than Ferier, Elfie was the oldest

truck in Carsville. 'I'm up!' Ferier said yawning. 'Look! I'm wide awake' he said

flashing his headlights. He had been out playing with his friends and wanted

to sleep in but knew his uncle wouldn't let him sleep in. With his uncle, you

could count on a big bucket of water being used to wake you up. Ferier revved

his engine and his dusty old blanket fell off him. Satisfied that Ferier was up

Elfie reversed himself. 'Your parents are out of town and you can help me in the garage today. A couple of folks are coming in for a check-up and you can help me with the tools' he said as he exited Ferier's room.

Ferier was little red car who was known for being the fastest. Born to two sports cars, Ferier was not only speedy but his buff body allowed him to develop strength as well. Ferier just couldn't wait to grow up because he knew he would be the fastest racer on the tracks. He glided down the hallway and went for a quick wash. Washed and shiny, he smiled in the mirror admiring himself. As he drove out to the street, he gleamed in the sunlight. He put on his shades and drove out of the garage to help his Uncle Elfie at Elfie Motors.

'Oh Elfie! I just can't seem to keep it in' an old green car said as it coughed. The car was dented in more places than Ferier could count and moved slowly because of its weak joints. 'Hello Mr. Mazda' Ferier said driving next to his uncle to see what the problem was with Mr. Mazda. As old and unwell as he usually was, Mr. Mazda was a regular visitor at Elfie motors.

BELCCCHHHH!

Mr. Mazda threw up black smoke. As the smoke cleared, Ferier saw the oil that had leaked from Mr. Mazda. 'Oh Boy!' Mr. Mazda blushed, embarrassed at his accident. Ferier tried not to giggle as his uncle glared at him. 'Not to worry

29

Maz!' his uncle said as Ferier pulled a hose to clean up the mess while Mr. Mazda drove up to the inspection spot. Just as he was done clearing the oil, his uncle fixed Mr. Mazda making sure he wouldn't leak any more oil.

'Hi Ferier!' his friend Merc said driving upto the garage. Merc was a fancy black car. Merc and Ferier had been friends since they were little kids. 'Hey Mr. Elfie' he said to his uncle. 'Are you making him work on our day off from school?' he asked pulling out a box of treats. 'Oh what are those?' Ferier asked quickly going to inspect the box. 'It's not for you. It's for your uncle' Merc said turning. 'Mother sent this for you. She said you had some gel for her?' he asked and Mr. Elfie laughed lightly. 'Your mother spoils me' he said kindly. Grabbing the box, he drove to the back of the garage where Ferier knew were all the important gels and tonics. Ferier had been banned from going there ever since he had crashed in a shelf of tools. Remembering the pain of at least hundred hammers dropping on his head, Ferrier was all too happy to avoid the back.

'Psst!' Merc said sliding next to Ferier. 'Your parents are gone and so are Ferdie's and Wolksie's. There is a new track open in the next town. We are planning to go there and race' Merc said and Ferier frowned. He really wanted to go with his friends but he hated breaking rules. 'Elfie will be so upset with me' Ferier said. 'He won't even find out. Plus my older sister is coming with a bunch of her friends so it won't just be us kids' Merc said and Ferier considered. 'Think about it' Merc said as Elfie glided out with a bottle of gel. 'Here you go kiddo!' he said giving Merc the gel. Ferrier was still deep in thought as more cars came in for check-ups and repairs.

He helped his uncle change a tyre, change some oil, check tyre pressure and fix some wipers. He had the most fun with Arnold, a four wheeler who had returned from a trip in the mountains and was covered in dirt from head to toe. 'Oh Arnold! Have mercy on my old parts' Alfie said Arnold drove in grinning. 'Oh Alf! It was the best trip I've had. I got to race with the friends and we camped under the open night sky. A car needs that. We're built to be out travelling' Arnold said as Elfie laughed. 'How am I going to clean you up?' Elfie asked. Arnold simply winked as he got ready for his power wash.

Ferrier thought about Arnold's words and made up his mind. He was going to go race with his friends under the night sky and have the best adventure of his life. He happily helped Elfie with the rest of the work. The afternoon passed quickly as cars kept coming one by one. Tired from a day of hard work, Ferier began to yawn as they cleaned up the shop. Ferier watched his uncle put the

31

tools away and before long his eyes began to droop. 'You can sleep after dinner' Elfie said. On the way home, they stopped to fill their tanks. With fuel filled to the brim, Ferrier felt energised again, all signs of sleep gone. He followed Elfie to their house. Ferrier's parents had designed the house so they could enter any room easily. With trail going to every room, the house had bridges and underpasses: everything to make a car's movement easy.

'I'll be in the guestroom' Elfie called and Ferrier grinned. Guest room faced away from the street and was the furthest from Ferrier's room which was closest to the road. 'Sure uncle' Ferrier said pretending to yawn. Once in his room, he began to pace. Minutes passed and slowly silence fell on the street outside.

TAP! TAP!

Ferrier crept to his window to see his friends Merc, Ferdie, Wolkskie , Rolly and Rover outside. They stood with their headlight dimmed not wanting to draw any attention. Keeping his own lights off, Ferrier quietly crept outside letting the streetlights aid him. 'We are to meet my sister near the town sign' Merc whispered when Ferrier reached them. Slowly, they left the street not daring to make a sound.

'That was so scary' Rolly said loudly as they reached the town sign towards the edge of their town, causing Ferrier to jump. A little scared, Ferrier had continued to check his rear view mirror afraid someone would be following them. Looking around, he saw no one. It reassured him but scared him a little as well. He had never been out without adults at this hour.

'Where is your sister?' Ferdie asked Merc, sounding scared. Just then, headlights flashed behind them and a group of older cars joined them. 'Alright kids! Ready to have fun?' Merc's sister, a blue convertible asked. Loud music blared and the younger cars cheered in excitement. 'The track isn't far from here. Just follow us' she said and everyone followed her.

The night sky was crisp and a gentle breeze kept them cool. With a full moon, the landscape was dimly lit. Shaking to the beat of the music, they crossed the farms. Bright, white lights lit in the distance as the tracks came into view. 'Woooottt! Wooooott!' Merc hooted excitedly as they sped up.

The cars stopped near the entrance as Merc's sister Mersa spoke to the guards. After speaking to them , she signaled at them to follow her. Ferrier's jaw dropped as he entered the tracks. The track stretched for miles as it curved and turned. Ferrier could feel the smooth tarmac under his wheels, he hadn't driven on anything smoother. 'Oh Boy!' he said as he looked at the empty stadium seats around the tracks. 'This is so cool!' Ferdie said in excitement.

'Ready to race or are you just going to admire it from a distance? Mersa asked and everyone changed gears. Ferrier felt the wind racing and he sped up. As he went faster and faster, his vision cleared and he could see every detail in front of him. From the road markings to the finest texture of the road. He had never felt more alive. 'Got you!' Merc shouted as he sped past Ferrier laughing. 'Oh no you didn't!' Ferrier yelled, speeding up even more.

Going around the tracks twice, they came to a stop near the exit. 'That was something else' Ferrier said as he braked near his friends. 'Time to go home' Mersa said as they talked excitedly amongst themselves. 'That was the coolest thing ever' Wolsie said. Chatting loudly, they began to drive back home.

'I'm hungry' Merc said and Mersa laughed.' You are always hungry' she complained. They continued the drive back, feeling the tiredness settling in. Ferrier couldn't wait to sleep in tomorrow.

'The town is just a mile from here. Can you all manage?' Mersa asked and everyone nodded. Ferrier couldn't wait to go to bed. Reassured, Mersa left with her friends and the kids made their way towards town. 'I'm hungry' Merc complained again as they neared the town sign. 'We're going home. Just a little further' Rolly said but even as he encouraged Merc, Ferrier could see him slowing down. 'Guys! My tanks empt-' Merc said before he came to a stop directly under the town sign.

'Oh no!' 'Merc!' 'You can't stop now' they all shouted in worry but Merc couldn't move an inch. 'Why didn't you eat before leaving' Ferrier asked worried. 'What will we do now?' he said looking around to see if Mersa was close by but it was only them standing in the middle of the road late at night. Ferrier had known this was a bad idea from the beginning.

'Don't worry! I've got a bottle that I can fill for Merc' Rolly said as they all sighed in relief. Within minutes, Rolly filled a bottle with thick golden liquid from his own tank that Merc guzzled down. 'All good!' Merc said laughing. 'Now all I need-' he began.

COUGH! COUGH! COUGH!

Before he could even finish his sentence he began to cough. Coming to a standstill, everyone watched in shock as Merc continued to cough, his body shaking violently.

'Aller-cough-gic-cough-reac-cough-tion' Merc managed as his headlights began to flash in panic.

'Oh no! Oh no! Oh no!' Rolly said panicking.

'What did you?' Ferrier asked terrified.

'Merc is allergic to diesel!' Rolly said and Ferrier gasped.

'What do we do? What do we do?' Wolksie asked, tears streaming down his face.

They all looked at each other knowing they were in trouble. Fear showed on every face. Terrified, they all pressed their alarms.

TEEEEEEEEEEEENNNNN!

TEEEENNN! TOOOOOONNN! TEEEEEEN! TOOOOOONNN!

TTRRRRRRR! TRRRRRR! TRRRRRRRRR!

As the alarms blared signaling an emergency, they continued to soothe Merc waiting for help to arrive.

Within minutes, they spotted headlights in the distance as adults arrived. Cars began to line up to see what was happening and what a sight it was!

Children out in the dark! A kid having an allergic reaction! Children out without adults!

Rushing to Merc, uncle Alfie and Mercs parent's took one look at him and connected him to the ambulance. 'Follow Rolly's parents home' Uncle Elfie said to the rest of the kids. Following the adults in silence the children waited to hear news of their friends.

Hours passed but no sleep came to them now. Finally, the gate to Rolly's house opened and in came everyone's parents, their faces disappointed.

'It wasn't-'

'We were-'

'Sorry but-'

'The track-'

'Mersa said-'

They all launched in explanations as the parents lined in front of them. Finally uncle Alfie spoke.

'You kids have no idea of the danger you put yourselves in. Sneaking out at night? Without adults? I have never heard or seen anything more absurd' Uncle Elfie said.

'We do everything for you kids and you still felt the need to cheat us' Ferdie's mother said tears rolling down her face.

'We just wanted an adventure' Ferrier said quietly, tears welling up in his eyes.

'And you will son. All of you will go on adventures by yourselves, with your friends and they will be the best adventures. But until you are old enough to learn more and know better, you should trust us to keep you all safe' Ferrier's father said gently.

'We only make the rules for your safety. If you kids want something, ask us. We will find a way for you to have it that doesn't put anyone at risk' Rolly's father said and the children nodded.

And so, as Merc got better, the children went with their families to the tracks and what an adventure they had.

IZZIE AND ALEX

Izzie sat brushing her doll's hair waiting for her parents to get back from work.

Sitting in her bedroom, with green walls and plants on every surface, Izzie had

organized her toys to pass the time. 'Oh how I wish I had a sibling' six year old

Izzie said for the hundredth time. After brushing her doll's hair and placing it

next to her collection of cars, she check if her plants needed water. After what

felt like hours, she heard the car horn outside. 'Mom! Dad!' she shouted

excitedly as she ran downstairs. Her mother walked in and hugged her after

hanging up her coat. 'Oh! I missed you two so much' Izzie said, getting her

mother's bag. 'We missed you too honey' her mother said as both her parents kissed her on the forehead. Waiting for them to change, Izzie ran to the kitchen to help the cook with their dinner.

With the table set, Izzie sat waiting. Sighing she got up and went up the stairs to her parents' room. 'Mom! Dad!' she called out again as her parents got out of their room with their clothes changed. 'Sorry love' her father said, picking her up. 'I'm always waiting for you' Izzie complained as they finally settled around the dining table. With dinner being served, Izzie launched into the story of her day and filled them in on every detail. 'I wish you were around more often' she said sadly in the end. Her mother reached out grabbing her hand.

'Hmm! What else do you wish for?' she asked smiling. 'I wish you and dad were around more often and when you'd be gone I had someone other than Ms. Fiona to keep me company so I wish I had a sibling to play with' Izzie said thinking. 'Is there anything we can do about it Steve?' her mother asked her father smiling as he frowned, pretending to think. Izzie looked at them in confusion trying to understand their mood. 'Maybe there is' her father finally said and Izzie stared at them suddenly excited. 'Am I going to have a baby sister?' she yelled. 'Or even a brother, I don't really care' Izzie asked, her eyes glowing. 'Settle down missy. Not a baby sibling but what if you had a sister your own age?' her mother asked. Thinking of a long lost twin, she cried out in excitement 'A sister my own age? Yes please!'.

Laughing lightly her parents helped her settle before continuing. 'No long lost twin' they said as if reading her mind. 'Then?' Izzie asked, frowning. Now she was really confused! 'You want a sister?' her father asked her and she nodded. 'What if there was someone who needed a sister as well. Would you like to be her sister?' her mother asked carefully as Izzie thought. 'Would she want to be my sister?' she asked thinking of all the toys she could share. 'Yes. She would' her mother said. 'But what about her own siblings or family. Would they let her be my sister?' Izzie asked.

'Well, we will be all the family she would have' her mother said causing Izzie to shoot out of her chair. 'She doesn't have a family of her own?' Izzie asked, her heart feeling for the girl as her mother shook her head. 'Not unless we become her family' her mother explained.

'Are you sure you are ready for a sister?' her father asked her again and Izzie nodded. Her parents then explained to her when and how her sister would arrive along with the system they had figured out so one of the parent spent more time at home. Izzie thought she was floating with happiness as she made her way to the bedroom. She was going to get both her wishes!

The next day, she helped her mother set up the spare bedroom as they waited for the call that would tell them about Izzie's new sister's arrival. Izzie had already set toys aside for her to give her when she arrived but the week passed without any call. As another week passed, Izzie prayed for her sister to arrive quickly. One Saturday, she sat with her parents having breakfast when the phone rang. Her mother answered and Izzie watched as her face brightened. Izzie's eyes widened in excitement as she understood it was the call they had been waiting for.

'Her name is Alex and she'll be here in a couple of hours' her mother exclaimed and Izzie jumped from the table. She had so much to do! She re-organized the dolls for Alex. With everything done, she stood at the door of Alex's bedroom wondering is there was something else she could do to make the place perfect for her sister.

The hours passed in a blur as they fixed the house and got ready. The bell finally rung and three rushed to the door. Standing there with an older woman was a girl younger than Izzie. With dark brown hair to Izzie's blonde, Izzie noticed Alex's green eyes to her blue. While she stood wearing her best powder blue frock, Alex wore simple jeans. 'Hi Alex!' Izzie's mother said kindly leading them inside the home. 'Izzie why don't you show Alex her room' her mother suggested and Izzie quickly nodded. Lifting two large black polythene bags, Alex quietly follow Izzie up the stairs. 'Here's mum and dad's room' Izzie said pointing out the doors. ' This is my room and this is yours' she said arriving at Alex's door.

'Your stuff?' Izzie asked and Alex lifted the black bags slightly. Quickly hiding her surprise, Izzie showed her around the room, pointing out all the things she had arranged for her. She expected Alex to tell her how much she loved them but Alex simply nodded. A little disappointed, Izzie went to her room. Pulling out the luggage bag identical to hers, she lifted out a pot of pink roses. Taking them to Alex's room, she knocked. 'Come in' a timid voice answered. 'These are for you' Izzie said self consciously as she left the luggage in the middle of the room and placed the roses on the window sill. 'This is our family luggage and we all have identical ones so you should have one too' Izzie explained as Alex continued to stare at her. 'And the pink roses are for you because pink means forever' Izzie said, looking at her feet. 'That's us' she continued waiting for a response but Alex remained silent. 'Right' Izzie finally said, leaving.

Despite all the excitement at her arrival, weeks passed but Alex hardly spoke to Izzie. They went to the school together but despite Izzie's efforts, Alex did not talk much, let alone play with her. 'Can we get some other sister who will play with me?' Izzie asked quietly as she sat with her parents. They were sitting in the living room sofa watching the television while Alex was upstairs. 'Izzie?' her mother asked her gently. 'I've tried everything since she came but she just won't play with me or talk to me. Can we get someone else?' Izzie asked sadly. 'I noticed you gave her your pink roses' her mother asked instead. Izzie nodded vigorously. 'Pink means-?' her mother asked. 'Forever' Izzie said quietly. 'Family is forever. What's a little time for adjustment when you have a forever to play together' her mom said and Izzie nodded.

With renewed enthusiasm, Izzie waited patiently for Alex to talk to her. Sometimes they exchanged a couple of words but mostly there was silence. One night, Alex was sitting in her bedroom with their parents gone when there was a gentle knock on her door. 'Come in' she called and Alex walked in with a couple of her books in hand. She was wearing a pair of round glasses that Izzie had never seen before.

'I hope I'm not bothering you' Alex said timidly. 'There's this question I need help with' she said raising her book. Jumping to help her, Izzie took her books. The girls began to ponder over Alex's homework. Before long they began to giggle at the silly errors Alex had made. 'I didn't know you wore glasses' Izzie said looking at Alex after they were done. 'Sometimes. When I get headaches' Alex admitted scrunching her nose as her glasses began to slide down making Izzie laugh. Just then they heard the car honk and Izzie ran downstairs. As she reached the bottom step, she realized Alex hadn't followed her. Sighing, she went to greet her parents reminding herself they had forever to do these things together.

'We are planning to go on a hike tomorrow' their parents announced to Izzie's delight. After packing her own things, she decided to check with Alex if she needed anything. Knocking gently, she found Alex sitting in the middle of her bed, with clothes strewn everywhere. 'I don't know what to pack. I've never been on a hike before' Alex admitted making Izzie smile. The evening passed with the two deciding what to pack and what to leave behind.

The next morning, the girls excitedly climbed into the car, ready for their road trip. Izzie played games while Alex contributed a little as well. Reaching the base of the trail, they got out and put on their backpacks. Izzie looked around at the rocky base of the hill. The trail was a thin dirt path hidden between the trees. The trees here grew taller than any Izzie had seen before. 'I'll lead and your mother will be at the back. We stay together. Once we reach the top, we'll have a barbecue there but if someone gets hungry, we have sandwiches' Izzie's father explained and so they began.

The narrow path widened in places as the distance between the trees grew more. They rested on the flatter rocks on the way to catch their breath. Izzie stayed close to Alex as the little girl struggled at little at some points. They climbed further, chatting and laughing.

'What is that, Lilly?' Izzie's father called to her mother as she walked ahead to inspect what her father was showing. Izzie paused to drink some water. As her parents resumed the hike, Izzie followed them. A couple of turns later, she looked back to see Alex was lagging. Assuming she was just round the corner, Izzie waited. Her parents continued to hike, lost in conversation. Not wanting to lose sight of them, Izzie walked backwards, to see what was keeping Alex. She turned the corner and her heart began to race. Alex was not behind them!

'Mom! Dad!' Izzie cried out as she continued to walk downhill, looking for Alex. 'Mom! Dad! Alex!' Izzie shouted. Her parents came rushing to her. 'Where's Alex?' Izzie asked, her eyes wide with fear. Quickly they began to climb downhill shouting out for Alex. Izzie turned a corner, there, sitting next to a big rock was the huddled figure of her sister.

'Oh Alex!' Izzie ran hugging her sister. Alex was rocking forward and backward, crying silently. 'I thought you had left me' Alex said between sobs. 'We would never leave you' Izzie said horrified. 'Oh girls!' their mother hugged them, her face pale with horror. 'We thought you were close by' she said hugging her little girls.

'I thought you didn't want me and were going to leave me here' Alex cried again but Izzie held her tightly, stroking her hair. 'You are my sister. You are family and family is forever' Izzie said, holding on to her tightly as her mother nodded in agreement, her arms wrapped around both her girls.

As everyone calmed down, they decided to have the barbecue right around the next turner at some flat rocks. Throughout that time, Izzie refused to let go of

Alex's hand and Alex was all too happy to let her bigger sister hold her. As the smell of grilled chicken rose in the air, the family began to laugh and chat, forgetting their worries, just a family having a good time.

LILLY THE PENGUIN

'Weeeeeeeee!' Lilly Penguin laughed as she slid down the ice.

'Weee!Ee!Eee!Eeee!' she sang as she rolled on the ice coming to settle in her mom's feet. Winter was around the corner and the sharpness of cold had increased. The clouds were more grey and the ice had stopped melting. But above all, the winds had changed direction. 'I can't wait for winters' Lilly jumped, flapping her little wings, trying to fly. 'Oh my first winters' she said staring dreamily into space.

'Oh dearie!' her neighbor Mrs. Delva laughed at her expressions. 'To be young and wish for winters' she said shaking her head. 'What does that mean?' Benty, Mrs. Delva's son asked as he slid around in the ice with Lilly. 'Look around and take it all in. For once the winters arrive, everything changes' Mrs. Delva said

solemnly. Listening to her, Lilly inhaled deeply, taking it all in when-

AAAACHOOOO!

She sneezed, her body falling backwards.

'Whoooaaaaaaaaaa!' she cried out as she slid backwards.

'There! There!' her father said scooping her up on his feet. 'Pappa!' Lilly cried

out snuggling. 'And what's going on here?' he asked, caressing her head with

his beak. 'Mrs. Delva asked me to take it all in before winters arrived' Lilly

explained as they made their way back up where Lilly's mother worked on their

igloo. 'Don't take it in like that silly' Lilly's mother Helen said affectionately.

'Look around you!' she said and Lilly did.

'Look at the Sun high in the sky, coloring it. See those beautiful shapes of the

clouds' her mother pointed and Lilly looked up. The sky was a pale blue, with

the sun a dull orange. 'See how everything is blue and gold. The penguins are

out playing and working together. The children are laughing and even babies

like you are sliding around' Helen said and sure enough. On every side of the snow road were igloos and families played around them. Children lay making snow angels around the igloos and Lilly smiled seeing all her friends happy.

'Once winters arrive here, the sky turns a sad grey. The wind gets so cold and sharp that little penguins won't be seen anywhere outside. And it snows so much that no one comes outside' her father explained and Lilly shuddered. 'But what will we do pappa if not play?' Lilly asked a little sad. 'We make our igloos super strong ' he said gentling kissing her momma on the forehead as she built their home. 'We stock up on fish to last the entire season' he said pointing to the bucket of fish at his feet , full to the brim. 'And we listen to stories around a nice fire' he said lifting Lilly up in the air causing her to giggle.

'Come on Benty' Lilly said, walking towards the road. 'Where are we going?' Benty asked following her. 'We are going to take it all in' she said seriously, causing everyone to laugh. The two babies wobbled around the road looking at everyone's houses. Some had added decorations to their igloos while others had made theirs bigger. Lilly and Benty made a stop at everyone's house saying hi to their friends, while inspecting decorations at others. 'What do you think this might be?' Lilly whispered to Benty as they stared at a sculpture their neighbor Mr. Allison had added in front of his house. The sculpture was circular with a ball on one side and two balls on the other.

'It's a ball with its friends?' Benty suggested as Lilly tilted her head to get a better look.

'It an igloo with more igloos on its side?' Lilly said seriously.

'Oh kids! How wonderful to see you' Mrs. Allison said waddling out of her house. 'Mr. Alison completed this sculpture and isn't it just wonderful?' she asked and the kids nodded wondering just what could be so wonderful about the it.

'What is it?' Benty asked just as Lilly stomped on his foot, telling him to be quiet.

'It's me of course' Mrs. Allison said simply as Benty roared with laughter. 'That's you?' he asked laughing and Lilly continued to pinch him.

'Absolutely wonderful' Lilly smiled forcibly as she dragged a laughing Benty away.

'That looks nothing like her' Benty laughed, rubbing his wing where Lilly had pinched him.

'But we shouldn't be rude' Lilly explained as Benty protested.

'You should listen to the smart young penguin' a voice said and both the kids turned.

'Uncle Kruger!' The kids yelled in delight, running to the old Penguin. Uncle Kruger was the oldest Penguin in town. With a drooping beak and wrinkles everywhere, he had stolen every kid's heart with his warm smile and even warmer stories that he served with hot cocoa.

'Now what are you two doing here?' he asked as the kids hugged him. 'We are admiring our little town before winters arrive and we are all forced inside' Benty said and Uncle Kruger nodded thoughtfully. 'And what have you seen?' he asked, interested as the children launched in their stories. They told him all about the colors of the sky, the winds and the changes in neighborhood. 'So now momma is fixing the igloo, making it super strong while Pappa is fishing so we have lots and lots to eat for winters' Lilly concluded, looking at the bucket at Kruger's feet similar to her father's. However, unlike her father's there was barely any fish in it.

'Why aren't you stocking up?' Lilly asked concerned as Uncle Kruger quickly moved the bucket out of Lilly's sight. 'Well Lilly! I'm an old man now' he said shrugging. 'I just can't fish enough now' he explained. 'But what if you run out' Lilly asked, her concern growing. 'In that case, I will run to you' Uncle Kruger said tickling Lilly but Lilly couldn't shake off the worry. If winters were as harsh as they said then Uncle Kruger wouldn't be able to run anywhere. Worried, she thought about Uncle Kruger all night.

The next morning she had an idea!

All through her classes, Lilly could barely sit still with excitement. Finally, as the bell rung to signal the end of the day, she quickly got to her feet. 'Hold up everyone' she called out to her friends and the little penguins looked at her curiously.

'We the baby penguins have been presented with a problem and we must find a solution to it' Lilly called out, startling everyone.

'Who here loves Uncle Kruger?' she asked and all hands shot to the air.

'Uncle Kruger was the first friend we all had. He showered us with love, stories and hot cocoa' Lilly said and everyone nodded their heads. 'Now he needs our help' Lilly declared.

'He is old and is not able to fish for himself' Lilly said. 'If he doesn't stock up on fish for winters, he will go hungry and we won't be able to help him then but we can help him now!' Lily said.

'I don't want Uncle Kruger to be hungry. He can have my lunch' Little Zaviar said sadly.

'I have a plan!' Lilly announced. 'If all of us work together, we can help stock up for Uncle Kruger. Now we can either ask for one fish each from our parents, or we can go fishing with them and fish for Uncle Kruger' Lilly said everyone nodded. 'I can ask my momma for three fish' Jacob said pointing to his round belly, causing everyone to laugh.

Lilly, Benty, Zavier, Jacob and half of their classmates went fishing with their fathers over the weekend. 'I bet I'll catch a huge pile' Lilly whispered to Benty as her father attached some bait to her pole. Excitedly she threw the line, waiting to catch the biggest fish. But minutes passed and the children began to grow bored. 'This is so boring' Benty complained causing everyone to laugh. 'Well, time passes quickly if you tell stories' Lilly's father suggested and Lilly thought of a story to tell. Just then she felt a tug on her line. 'I've got something' she said excitedly as she struggled to hold on to the fishing line. 'Gotcha' her father said, as he helped her reel the fish in.

The children abandoned their own lines and ran to see Lily's catch. 'That's so big' Benty admired as everyone else nodded. 'I can't wait to catch mine' Benty said running back to hurriedly pick his line. With renewed enthusiasm the children began to wait. 'What will you do with such a big catch' Lilly's father asked her. 'It's a present for someone' she smiled. Before long Benty called out, announcing his first catch. 'Mine is bigger' he said with a satisfied look on his face as Lilly rolled her eyes. 'It is not' she said ignoring him and returning to her line.

By the time they made their way back, Lilly had caught five fish, Zavier six and Benty one. 'We'll see you at home' Lilly said to her father, motioning for the rest of the kids to follow her. Wobbling under the weight of their buckets, the children met in the park. 'Okay so! What's the progress update?' Lily asked. 'I'm done making our own little igloo' Jemimah said proudly, pointing to a little storage space they had made for the fish. 'I caught five and asked my father for three more' Lilly said proudly. 'I got ten fish' Jacob said proudly . One by one, the children emptied their buckets. Feeling exceptionally proud with themselves, they went back home.

The next day, the children caught an even larger pile of fish. The adults stared at them curiously as the babies carried their fish to the park. Thinking they were having a party the adults went about their work. As evening fell, everyone stared in wonder as baby penguins began to make their way to Mr. Kruger's house. Walking in straight lines, wobbling from right to left, they carried their buckets full of fish and placed them outside his house. Everyone gathered to see what was happening as the children waited for Mr. Kruger to return home.

'Now what's going on here?' Mr. Kruger asked, seeing the crowd outside his house. Everyone parted silently for him to pass, curious to see what would happen. 'What-?' Mr. Kruger said in surprise.

His entire front lawn was covered with buckets and buckets of fish!

'We know you've gotten old and can't fish as much now so we decided to fish for you' Lilly said as Mr. Kruger stared in amazement, lost for words. 'We didn't want you to get hungry' Benty said. Mr. Kruger continued to stand in awe as the children then helped carry the fish to his store. 'It's still not full to the top' Lilly said sadly as they overturned the last bucket.

'Let me see if we can do something about it' her father said kindly. Following the kid's example, the adults made their way to Mr. Kruger's store and overturned their own buckets until it was full to the top. 'Well! That should help you last for not one but two winters' Lilly's father said laughing.

'The winters might get cold but not so much when you have such great children to warm your heart' Mr. Kruger said as he invited all the children for a hot cup of cocoa. Soon they were out of space in his little igloo. 'We can go to the park' Zavier suggested. Before long, the children sat in a circle with their parents joining them as Mr. Kruger told them stories. The entire neighborhood enjoyed themselves as the community came together, the young and the old to care for one another.

MASHA'S CHRISTMAS

In the city of Toothspolk, lived a young girl named Masha. With curly brown hair and kind brown eyes, Masha loved to play with her ball, play dress up with her dolls and above all, she loved Christmas. Every year, she would wait for winters for it was her favorite season. Winters also meant that Christmas was around the corner. 'I have made the biggest list of presents' she announced one morning in December. Running down the stairs with her curls bouncing, she dragged her blanket along with a piece of paper and her bright blue pencil. 'I'm sure Santa will be extra happy to get you your presents' her father, picking her up, causing her to giggle. 'What's on the list?' he asked as she quickly hid it from view. 'It's only for Santa's eyes' she said wagging her finger at her father who laughed in response.

Hurriedly getting dressed for school, Masha walked to her class with a spring in her step. She sat through first period English, paying extra attention so she wouldn't begin day dreaming about Christmas. 'Class! We will be working in partners' her teacher Ms. Patty announced. Masha loved working with people because it gave her a chance to make new friends and learn so many new things. Ms. Patty began to call out names from her list to the sound of scraping chairs as students began to move around to sit next to their partners.

'Masha and Sara' Ms. Patty announced and Masha excitedly looked around to see the girl she had never spoken to much. Sara was a quiet girl who kept to herself. With thick black hair roughly tied in a ponytail and tired eyes, Masha had always seen Sara come late to classes and be the first one to leave. Now she waved at her pointing to the empty seat next to her. Slowly, Sara made her way to Masha and sat next to her. Noticing the rumpled clothes that hadn't been ironed and unpolished shoes Masha hoped that the girl and her family was okay. Masha had only once come to school with unpolished shoes and that had been when her mother had fallen sick.

'Hi! I'm so excited' Masha told her but Sara simply nodded. ' Now students' Ms. Patty clapped her hands to get everyone's attention. 'You have to write an essay on one of the parks in the town that will be due just before Christmas holidays' she explained and Masha's ears perked up. 'You will pick a park and write about what you like and dislike about it and ways to make it better' she said. 'If we send it to Santa, maybe his elves will make it just the way we like it' a boy spoke up causing everyone to laugh.

'Which park do you want to pick?' Masha asked Sara who just shrugged, folding her arms on the desk and resting her head on them. 'I like one next to the supermarket. It's close to the school, has a skating rink and you can always go to the supermarket if you get hungry' Masha said smiling as Sara yawned. 'Are you bored?' Masha asked, offended. 'What? No!' Sara said quickly lifting her head. 'That park sounds fine' Sara said as she tried to hide a yawn. 'If you're not bored then you can yawn all you want but don't let Ms. Patty see you' Masha said excited again causing Sara to smile.

'We can go to the park tomorrow after school and begin our essay. We'll see the people who visit and I can bring sandwiches for us to enjoy while we are there' Masha said already planning all their activities. She ran on her way back home excited to tell her parents about her new friend and the activities she had planned. 'Mom! Dad!' she called out excitedly as soon she opened the door. 'In here' she heard her father. Following his voice to the living room, her eyes rounded in excitement. The floor was littered with brown boxes full of Christmas decorations. 'Oh boy! Oh boy! Oh boy!' Masha cried out in excitement. 'We'll get our tree this weekend but decided to take out the decorations now' her mother explained but all Masha could focus on were the colorful decorations. After unpacking, they pulled out a box of photographs. Cuddling on the sofa between her parents, Masha went through the photographs.

'Oh I absolutely adore this one' her father said pointing to the one with the three of them lying in the snow with the remains of a snowman. Masha remembered that day so clearly. She had built a snowman with her mother while her father had gone looking for a ski cap for the snowman's head. Just as they had tried to fit the cap on its head, the head had exploded in a shower of snow which had marked the start one of the craziest snow fights. 'I love this one as well' her mother said as the continued to go through the pictures. After finishing going through the photographs, her father got sandwiches from the kitchen while Masha picked out a movie to watch with her mother. Settling in with her parents, the day passed blissfully as the sky darkened outside bringing fresh snow.

The next day, Masha made her way to sit with Sara who was gently dosing off with her head resting on her arms again. Masha quietly sat down, pulling out her notebook. 'Sara' she whispered as Mr. Jefferson arrived for first period. 'Sara!' she whispered again as the girl jolted awake. 'Oh no!' she said looking around panicked. 'Did I dose off again?' she asked, trying to fix her hair with her hands. 'It's okay. He just arrived' Masha reassured her as Sara realized the teacher had arrived.

'Are you okay?' Masha asked her new friend. 'Yeah! Yeah!' Sara nodded absently.

The day passed without incident with the two girls talking little. 'Are you ready?' Masha asked Sara lifting her bag and Sara looked at her confused before she remembered. 'Oh absolutely!' she smiled reassuringly at Masha. The two girls walked together to the park after school.

'Isn't it just beautiful?' Mash asked. The park looked like a scene straight out of a fairytale. Snow covered every surface. The ground, bushes and trees. The fresh snow from last night lay undisturbed. With no visitors, it hadn't turned to a muddy slush that they saw everywhere else. 'It is something else' Sara said admiring the view. Glad to be dressed appropriately, the girls picked a bench close to the fountain that had frozen over, the water icicles sparkling in the day.

'So what do we love about the park?' Masha asked, pulling out her paper and pencil along with the sandwiches. Putting the sandwiches between them she began to write. 'The grocery store, the fountain, the distance from the school' Masha said writing down the points they had thought off. 'I love feeding the birds that come here the rest of the time of the year' Sara said, chewing on a sandwich as Masha wrote. 'I love the musicians who sit here to play in the evening filling every corner with the most wonderful notes' Masha said.

'I wish there were more swings here' Sara said looking towards the lonely swing set in the corner. It was usually impossible to get your turn when the park was full. 'Don't forget the shawarma guy with his stall' Sara said and Masha nodded. She loved his cheesy, spicy shawarmas. 'We forgot one thing' Masha giggled and Sara stared at her questioningly. 'The snow of course' she said and Sara giggled as well. 'But I love snow anywhere. I think it's because it means Christmas is here and I love everything about Christmas' Masha said excitedly but Sara just shrugged. 'Every year I get everything on my list' Masha said and Sara stared at her in wonder. 'You do?' she asked. 'Of course I do!' Masha said. 'I even finished my list for this year. I can't wait for Santa' she continued as Sara continued to stare at her. 'Santa never gets my list so I stopped making them' Sara said sadly as Masha stared in horror. How was it possible for Santa to miss a list?!

'How is that possible?' Masha asked standing up in shock. 'I used to make the list but Santa missed it every year' Sara said. 'Did you leave him cookies and milk?' Masha asked ready to get to the bottom of this. 'I would save all my cookies for Santa but he never found them. I even saved money to get him fancy ones but that didn't help' Sara said looking around, but not before Masha caught a shine of tears in her eyes. 'Maybe it's my dad's coughing that keeps him away. It does get very loud at night. He's a little unwell you see' Sara explained.

'Don't worry!' Masha said hugging her. ' One of his lazy elves must have missed your address. This year you give me your list and I'll put it with mine. Then Santa will know there is another kid here' she reassured Sara as her friend's face lit up. 'Don't be sad. Santa has a lot of making up to do' Masha said causing

Sara to laugh, all sadness gone. With the sun beginning to set, the girls made final notes before heading back to their homes.

That night, after dinner Masha sat on her bed in her pajamas, her list in front of her. Taking the pen, she crossed out her entire list and instead began to write on the backside.

Dear Santa!

Every year you bring me presents that I love very much but sir you have made a mistake. There is another little girl on my street. Her name is Sara and she is my friend, a really nice girl you see. One of your elves missed her out and she has not received any of the presents on her list. I know it wasn't your fault and the elf responsible will be told of his mistake (kindly please since it is Christmas) but you have a lot of making up to do. Since you will have to get all of the things for Sara to make up for lost years, it is okay if you don't bring my presents since there will be little space left in your sack. I will still leave the cookies that you enjoy so much!

Love,

Masha Stuart,

579-A

Addison Street

Toothspolk.

The next days passed in a blur as the girls finished their assignments. 'All done!' Masha said smiling as they submitted their essay. 'Now where's the list' Masha asked and Sara excitedly pulled out an envelope. 'Promise no looking?' Sara asked causing Masha to roll her eyes. 'Of course silly' she said. She carefully put Sara's list in her bag. Hugging her friend goodbye and wishing her a Merry Christmas, Masha ran home. She placed her letter in Sara's envelope and waited for Christmas eve. Playing in the snow with her family during the day and watching movies at night, Masha enjoyed her Christmas break. On Christmas eve, she left the letter with cookies and milk and went to bed smiling.

The next morning she woke up with the biggest smile on her face. 'Merry Christmas!' she shouted through the house and ran to the living room. 'What?' she asked surprised to see a pile of gifts for her. Her face fell slightly at the thought of Sara not getting her presents again. 'There's a special letter for you this year' her father said pointing to the envelope on top of her pile of presents.

Ho!Ho!Ho!

Dear Masha!

First of all a very Merry Christmas to you. It upset me greatly to find out a nice little girl didn't get her presents. The elf responsible was found and told to be extra extra careful. I am so proud and happy to know that there are such selfless girls like you in the world. I know you crossed out your list but I always bring an extra stash of toys for emergencies (there was a time when it rained on all my toys but that's a story for another time). Hope you have a wonderful Christmas.

Love,

Santa.

'Oh Boy! Oh Boy!' Masha jumped up and down excitedly as she began to open her presents. Surrounded by toys ,her father took a photograph of her with her letter from Santa and hung it proudly on the tree. Surrounded by her loved ones, Masha thought for the hundredth time, 'Oh how I love Christmas'.

RUFUS AND FURBALL

'Eric! Eric! Eric!' Furball chanted as her best friend Eric played with his ball.

'Eric! Eric! Eric!' she cheered, jumping up and down. Furball was a little grey

kitten with black stripes, the size of little Eric's hand. Despite her extremely

small size, she was cheering at the top of her lungs. 'Meow! Meow! Meow!' Eric

heard his biggest supporter cheer him on and kicked the ball with all his might.

'Goal!' Furball yelled and chased Eric as the two best friends ran after the ball

as it rolled downhill. Laughing, Furball sped up to keep up with Eric. They ran

past the flower shop, bakery and the shoe shop until the ball came to rest under

a tree. Eric slowed as he saw a figure rise from behind the tree.

'Rufus' Eric whispered to Furball, who in her excitement had sped past Eric and didn't hear the warning.

Rufus was one angry dog. His dark brown fur was matted with dirt in places and his tail was bent at an angle. With a bright red scar across his face and a constant frown, he scared anyone who dared to come too close. Eric stared in horror as Furball ran straight towards him.

'Woof! Woof!' Rufus barked angrily as he saw a little ball of fur roll in front of him. He was in angrier mood than usual. Some silly human had dropped a nail and Rufus had accidentally stepped on it. Eric saw his little kitten run towards the angry dog and he ran forward.

'Careful Furball!' Eric called out, warning her to keep her distance from the angry dog.

'Careful little Kitten' Rufus said as the kitten ran straight towards the other stray nails. 'Woof!' he barked and Furball stopped. Her little paw stopped mid air directly above a sharp, gleaming nail.

'Furball' Eric said reaching his kitten, quickly picking her up. With her safe in his arms, he looked up at Rufus. With his scar even more red up close and eyes that looked annoyed, Eric's legs trembled a little in his shorts. He carefully began to step away from the dog, while Rufus settled on the ground once again focusing on his hurting foot. Ignoring the scared boy, Rufus licked his wound. 'Thank you' a little voice said and Rufus looked up in surprise to see the tiny kitten waving at him.

'Whoa! That was close. You can't run off like this Furball. You could have gotten hurt' Eric said looking at Furball seriously. Furball stared at her favorite human and licked his face. She loved him with his short brown hair, round face and bright blue eyes. 'It was close' Furball agreed remembering the shiny tip of the nail. 'That's one scary dog. He would have eaten you in one bite' Eric said and Furball looked at him confused. 'That angry dog?' she asked and Eric nodded. 'He looks so scary and mean' Eric said and Furball laughed. 'He isn't scary. He saved me' Furball said but Eric shook his head. 'You're so little Furball. You don't know. He is one very dangerous dog' Eric said, settling on the grass as Furball curled in his lap. 'We should stay far away from him' Eric said scratching her behind the ears. Before Furball could protest, the scratching made her lazy distracting her.

A week passed and Furball decided she was no longer a little ball of fur. She was bigger than Eric's hand, could jump from window sills and could run up and down the stairs ten times without getting tired. One sunny afternoon, she sat in the windowsill looking at the street outside. The flowers were blooming in the gardens and babies went about in their buggies. The canaries were chirping and playing in their trees but Furball was stuck inside. Eric was still in school and Furball was so bored.

TING TONG!

The bell rang and the housekeeper Ms. Fiona opened the door. The deliveryman had arrived with boxes, Furball saw delighted. She couldn't wait to play with the boxes. Her face fell as she watched as Ms. Fiona put the boxes in the top cupboard, far away from Furball!

Sad, Furball looked around for something else to play with. Her eyes fell on her bright red ball. Before long, she began chasing the ball. She pushed it from the living room to the stairs, to the kitchen, back to the stairs. Before she knew it, the ball rolled out the open front door and out in the lawn. Lost in her game, Furball continued to chase the ball around the garden. Before long, she went out the garden and onto the road. 'Teeeeen! Tooooon!' cars honked past her as she looked up. Her eyes widened as she realized she was in the middle of the road.

Furball looked around and saw the inviting street stretching out in the warm sun. She looked back at the cold empty house with just Ms. Fiona and decided to play outside. She pushed her ball around and continued to chase it, laughing every time she caught it. 'It was so much more fun than just sitting inside' she decided as she chased her ball down an empty street.

'Alone little kitty?' a raspy voice asked and Furball looked up to find an eagle sitting on a mound of trash. Gulping, Furball looked around to see a very dirty street. Trash overflowed from trashcans, broken bottles rolled on the floor, nothing like the beautiful street she lived on.

'I-I was just playing' Furball said as an eagle swooshed down to sit on her ball. 'Why don't you play with us?' another eagle asked landing next to Furball. Furball looked at their pointy beaks and talons and shook her head. 'I should get home' she stuttered as the eagle got closer to her, filling her nose with a nasty smell.

'If I could have my ball back' Furball said, scared as another giant eagle landed behind her, blocking her exit. 'But we want to play' the first eagle said in a sing song voice. 'I- I would love to but I should get back home' Furball said as she saw the giant eagle sharpen its claws.

'My ball-' Furball began as the eagle dove towards her, it's sharp claws outstretched.

'MEOOOWWWWWW!' Furball screamed just as someone thundered down the street.

WOOFFFF! WOOOOFFFFF!

Furball looked up to see Rufus running down the street, causing the eagles to fly away instantly.

'What are you doing here alone? Rufus barked angrily. Furball saw the familiar bent tail, the angry scowl and bright red scar and ran towards him, hugging his leg.

'What-?' Rufus looked down confused as the little ball of fur hung from his leg. 'Oh Rufus! I am so glad to see you. Those eagles wanted my ball and they looked so mean' Furball said not letting go of his leg.

Unsure of what to do with the little creature attached to his leg, Rufus just stared in confusion.

No one had ever hugged him before!

'They wanted more than your ball' he said realising this silly ball of fur had no idea of the extent of danger she had been. 'Well I sure am glad they didn't take anything. You scared them just fine' Furball said and Rufus realised she had no intention of letting go.

'Why are you here all alone?' Rufus asked again. Furball forgot whatever she was going to say and looked around, gulping. 'I was playing with the ball and didn't see where I was going' she said timidly.

'And how do you plan to get back home? Rufus asked wondering how silly the boy was to let this tiny creature out of his sight. As far as Rufus could see, this ball of fur needed protection all the time.

'I didn't have a plan but now that you're here, you can take me home' Furball said and Rufus watched in shock as she climbed up his leg. Before he could say anything, she settled on his back. Rufus felt himself go very still. He couldn't remember someone being so trusting.

'Silly little ball of fur' he said, walking very careful, scared of Furball falling off his back.

'Rufus? Furball said as he turned to leave the dirty alley.

'Furball?' he asked.

'My ball?' she asked and Rufus sighed, a smile breaking across his face.

He moved to the bright red ball and nudged it with his nose. Together, they left the alley with Furball telling stories of her adventures with Eric and Rufus pushing the ball ahead of them with his nose.

'FURBALL!' Eric yelled as he spotted her with the scary dog. He had spent the past hour looking for her everywhere. 'Furball!' he ran to his kitten as she jumped into his arms. 'Oh Furball! I was so worried' he said, tears streaming down his face.

'I got distracted. Rufus here-' Furball began but Eric looked up angrily at the dog.

'Stay away from us!' he shouted at Rufus. Shocked, Rufus jumped away.

'Shooo!' Eric shooed Rufus away.

'That was my friend' Furball cried but Eric carried her inside. Furball continued to struggle as she saw Rufus standing in the shadows, her red ball forgotten.

Rufus stared at the little boy, as he carried Furball away. He continued to look at their retreating backs, his heart growing heavier. 'I live on the streets. I am tough' he reminded himself even as his heart ached in his chest. He continued to stand outside, waiting in case Furball came back. Finally as it grew dark, he turned around ready to leave. Just then, his eyes fell on Furball's red ball. Running to it, he woofed happily. He nudged it with his nose, pushing it forward.

'Woof! Woof!' he barked happily chasing the ball. Entering his alley, Rufus nudged the ball towards a pile of boxes. He removed the boxes to reveal his pile of treasures: his blanket, a chewed up teddy and now this red ball. Vowing to keep it safe for Furball, he tucked it neatly between some newspapers.

A week passed and Furball hadn't played with Eric even once. She hadn't played when he had given her a yellow ball. She had ignored the bright blue string that he had spread across the living room. But he was sure they would have a blast today. It was picnic day!

The family packed their basket and went to the town park. Furball jumped around in excitement at being outside after ages. She sniffed the sunflowers, the grass and the basket of food. Just as she neared the water pond, she saw the reflection of a familiar face with the red scar. However, just as she looked up she saw some boys chasing Rufus away. Angry at humans for being mean to her friend, Furball decided to follow the boys. As Eric chased a kite with his friends, Furball climbed over the chain link fence, across the pond and towards the trees.

She saw the boys chasing Rufus into the dense trees and followed them. As she neared, her eyes widened in horror. The boys held rocks in their hands as they chased poor Rufus. Furball couldn't let them hurt her friend! She chased the boys, running as fast as she could, climbing over the rocks, ready to jump over the boy when-

SMACK!

She tripped over the rocks. Tears streamed down her face as she realised she was a tiny kitten unable to help Rufus. She heard Rufus bark in the distance and worry gripped her heart. Wiping her face with a paw she ran back to the picnic spot.

'Help Eric! Help!' Furball meowed, pulling at Eric's trousers. 'Help Rufus!' Furball cried. Alarmed at seeing Furball in tears, Eric ran with her as Eric's friends followed them. Running to the boys, Furball saw they still had the rocks in their hand as Rufus continued to hide from them.

'Back off!' Eric shouted. The boys turned to see Eric with his large group of friends. 'Why are you hurting that poor dog? Get away from him' Eric shouted. 'We were just having fun' one boy said dropping the rock.

'How can hurting someone be fun? Get away from him' Eric said again as the boys dropped their rocks, running away. Furball ran up to Rufus as he limped out from behind a tree. 'You're hurt' Furball cried as Rufus lowered his head. As she hugged him tightly, Eric and his friends brought bandages from the first aid kit for Rufus. 'I'm sorry Rufus' Eric said walking up to Rufus. Gently, he wrapped a bandage around his leg. 'Now I understand why you were so angry all the time. I would be too if everyone treated me like this' Eric said.

As the Sun set, the children played with a little ball of fur and a dog with a scarred face learning the importance of treating animals with love and care.

THE FLU ON RAINBOW STREET

'Catch me if you can!' Zuma laughed as he ran with the frisbee held tightly in his mouth. 'Not fair!' his friend Donkey panted as he tried to keep up with his friend. Zuma was a little red Labrador who adored his little grey friend Donkey. They wore matching badges on their tails and did everything together. 'You stole the frisbee' Donkey complained. He had been readjusting the little blue disk in his mouth when Zuma had jumped in, running off with it. 'You will never be able to catch him Donkey, why bother?' their friend Gary the goat said joining them. 'You watch. One of these days' Donkey said panting heavily as he finally came to a stop near Gary. The children stood in the middle of their street playing. The narrow street had tall houses built close together. With a house of every color, they called it the rainbow road.

'Let play catch' Roco the Racoon said as he joined them with a bright green ball in his hand, with Sara Squirrel and Jasmine sheep by his side. Excitedly, they formed a circle and began to pass the ball around. Before long the peaceful game of catch turned into a fierce game of tag. Anyone who got hit by the ball would be tagged and had to sit out till the next game. Sounds of laughter filled the streets as the children ran and ducked, trying to stay clear of the ball that Donkey tossed.

His eyes fixed on Zuma, Donkey aimed carefully, grinning. 'He was going to get Zuma!' he thought. Tossing the ball high in the air, he watched as his aim went off. The ball went higher and higher until-

CRASH!

'Not Mr. Jeff' the children exclaimed together. But the ball went straight through his window, breaking the glass. Mr. Jeff Chicken was the scariest and angriest man on the street and children tried their best to stay clear of him. Looking at one another, they considered running away but with such close houses there really was no way of avoiding the scolding they were sure to get.

The door to his red house opened and out he came. His green feathers standing at their edge and a little black cap settled on his little brown head, Mr. Jeff chicken looked at them with annoyance. 'Why is it that whenever I consider lying down, it is always my house where your ball will land' he asked as the children hung their heads.

'Can we have our ball back Mr. Jeff Chicken? We promise to be more careful next time' Zuma said. 'That's the third time this week. Last time it was donkey who promised' Mr. Jeff chicken said staring at Donkey who was looking everywhere but at the angry chicken in front of him. 'The time before that it was Roco' Mr. Jeff said and it was Roco's turn to avoid Mr. jeff's eyes. 'And the time before that it was Jasmine who promised' Mr. Jeff said to which Jasmine quickly replied. 'We didn't break the window the other times' she pointed out.

'Why-is-it-always-my-house?' Mr. Jeff shouted causing the children to shrink even more. 'No more' he declared, turning around and returning to his house. Looking the closed door the children waited sadly for the ball. A couple of minutes passed and the door opened slightly. 'Here you go kiddos' Mrs. Jeff Chicken said, kindly giving the children their ball back.

Happy at having their ball back the children made plans of meeting after school to play more. Running to school, they made it just in time for the first class. Half the day went without incident. Donkey and Zuma sat passing notes to each other when the school speaker went on.

'Attention children!' they heard the principal. ' he school will now close until further notice. There is no need to panic. Please leave in an orderly fashion. The school buses are waiting outside for you. You are requested to avoid contact with one another'

Chaos erupted as children hooted at getting to leave school early. 'Quietly!' their teacher kept calling out but the excited children quickly packed their bags in a rush to get out of school. 'Is it like a post spring break?' Zuma asked Donkey excitedly as they ran out of the school. 'I don't care what it is! I can't wait to play tag!' Roco said, walking with them. Walking back home, laughing and joking, Zuma waved at Donkey and Roco as his house came first. 'I'll be back after lunch' he called out while others waved back at him. Donkey went home in the house next door, while Roco went in the house next to Donkey's.

They waved at each other one more time before heading inside their homes. 'Mom! You won't believe it!' Zuma shouted excitedly as he ran to the living room. He stopped short as he saw his mother's worried expressions and the bags of grocery on the table. 'Were they giving it out for free?' he attempted to joke, never having seen so many grocery bags together.

'Sit down Zuma' his father said and Zuma turned around surprised to see his father back from the office. Now he began to worry. 'What's going on?' he asked sitting down. 'Zuma there is a flu going around and we will have to stay home for two weeks' his mother said and Zuma grinned. What was a little flu. He couldn't wait to play ball all day for two weeks.

'I can't wait to go and play' Zuma said and his father intervened. 'You don't understand son. We can't leave the house for two weeks until we know for sure we haven't gotten the flu' his father said and Zuma frowned. 'But we get flu all the time. We can't possibly stay at home for two weeks' Zuma said thinking about the plans he had made to see his friends. 'Son. This isn't like other times' his father said.

'But I was going to meet Donkey and Roco just now' Zuma said, panicking a little. 'This flu is dangerous. Just two weeks son!' his father said. Zuma looked at his mother for reassurance but she simply hugged him tightly. Unable to believe his ears, he grabbed his bag as his parents turned on the telly. Standing in the doorway Zuma heard the news of the dangerous flu and people sick. Worried, he ran up to his room.

Ringggg! Riiingggg!

Donkey picked up on the first ring. 'Did you hear?' Donkey asked as soon as he answered. 'This is crazy. Let me add Roco and the gang' Zuma said as he added the rest of his friends. Everyone spoke at once as they connected, finally calming down it was Jasmine who spoke first.

'I'm scared' she admitted and everyone nodded. 'Has any of you sneezed?' Donkey asked as they all wondered when was the last time they had sneezed. 'Don't worry' Sara said. 'It's just two weeks. Then it will go back to normal' she said and everyone nodded, a little scared.

The week passed extremely slowly. The first day Zuma went through all his storybooks and organised them. Then he got to his clothes and organised them by color. Next came his sock drawers followed by the rest of the drawers. By the fourth day, he washed all his clothes. Day six came with organising the freshly washed clothes. By day seven, Zuma was bored and out of things to organise. The street outside remained empty as no one dared to go outside. He had begun to avoid the living room for the fear of scary news about the

85

dangerous flu. He called his friends regularly and soon they began to play games, watching each other on their little screens. As the second week, finally came to an end, Zuma's parents sat him down.

'I never thought I would say this but I can't wait to go back to school' Zuma said causing his mother to exchange a look with his father. 'School isn't opening just yet' his mother said hesitantly. 'I'm still stuck?' Zuma asked unable to believe his ears. 'The flu is still here and schools are risky' his father explained as ZUma's face fell. 'But you can play with your friends' Zuma's father explained and Zuma perked up. 'I can?' he asked happily and his father nodded. 'But you cannot go close to them. And you must wear a mask' his father said and Zuma frowned. Pulling out a box of masks, he helped Zuma put one on. The mask covered his tiny nostrils and mouth. 'It makes my whiskers itch' he complained causing his parents to laugh. 'We'll get through this together' his mother said, giving his face an affectionate lick.

Running out on all fours, Zuma watched excitedly as his friends came out with masks as well. Running to Donkey, he was about to hug him when he caught his dad's eye. 'Hi' he said from a distance, raising his front paw awkwardly. They all stared at each other for a while before deciding to play tag. Before long, the street was full of laughter and shouts again as the children tossed the ball. Aiming for Donkey, Zuma threw the ball with all his might. But it went higher and higher until-

CRASHHHH!

'Not Mr. Jeff Chicken!' the children exclaimed together. Like every time, they watched in horror as the door to his house opened. 'Where's Mr. Jeff?' the children asked confused as Mrs. Jeff came out with the ball instead. 'Mr. Jeff got the flu. He's unwell' Mrs. Jeff said. Before the children could say anything their parents sprang forward. 'Why are you out Mrs. Jeff. You will give everyone the flu!' Roco's mom asked worriedly as she dragged Roco back inside the house. Within minutes, the laughter was gone and the street stood empty once again with a lone green ball lying forgotten on the road.

'I can't believe he has the flu and she came outside like that' Zuma's mother complained. Zuma stared at his feet, his eyes filling with tears. He didn't want Mr. Jeff or anyone else to be sick and alone. 'Oh honey! You won't get sick' his mother quickly reassured him. but Zuma cried even more. 'What if I do mom? You said we will get through this together but we are not. If we fall sick will everyone else leave us alone like that?' Zuma cried, running up to his room. He missed his friends and school and playing outside!

There was a gentle knock on his door. Zuma quickly wiped the tears from his face with his paws. 'You were right son' his father said sitting on the bed with him. 'It is scary and we will get through it together' he said, 'Before you know it Mr. Jeff will be well as well' he said. 'How about we make a gift basket for Mr. Jeff that he can enjoy while he gets better' his mom suggested and Zuma nodded excitedly. He took his favorite book and new ball. Taking a card, he began to write.

Dear Mr. Jeff

We know you're a little unwell but I'm sure you will scare the flu away in no time. While you get better, we will try not to make any noise with the ball. This way you can sleep well and get better.

Love

Zuma

Together with his parents, Zuma put fruits and soup in a basket with other gifts. As they made their way to Mr. Jeff's house, Zuma saw other families coming with baskets as well. One by one they placed the baskets in front of Mr. Jeff's gate and returned to their homes. Standing in their doorways, they watched as Mrs. Jeff came out and took the baskets inside, her eyes filled with tears of joy.

The next day the children returned to the street to play with masks on. Instead of tag they played catch and chatted constantly.

The week passed quickly when they had each other. One fine afternoon they came outside and saw a basket full of balls waiting for them. They ran to the basket, inspecting the balls when the door to Mr. Jeff's house opened and out he came. His green feathers shining in the Sun. 'Mr. Jeff Chicken!' the children exclaimed happily. 'This time I thought I could play with you kids' Mr. Jeff laughed as he joined them, all recovered.

THE WOODPECKER'S VILLAGE

Deep in the rainforest of Amazonia, far from civilization, lived a community of woodpeckers. Among the deepest trees, with a river flowing nearby the woodpeckers lived happily. 'Peck and peck! Night and day we peck!' they sang as they went about their tasks. Among them lived Haris, a mischievous little woodpecker. He was known for his pranks and his good heart. To be pranked by Haris was an everyday thing and the woodpeckers were always keeping an eye out for him. 'I will get you' Harrypecker said after he had spent a couple of minutes pecking a piece of wood he was sculpting only to find out it had been a giant bar of soap. Rinsing his mouth with water, Harrypecker sprayed Haris with water making the little woodpecker laugh. Soaked from his little green head all the way to his blue claws, Haris took off, done with pranks for the day, ready for tasks.

However, there was someone who Haris loved pranking the most, who terrified everyone else. Near the river, away from the trees lived a giant green ogre by the name of Ronald. The ogre lived by himself. Every morning the ogre would get ready to begin his day's work with an eye out for Haris but Haris was always too quick for him. Swinging his giant green hands, he would chase a laughing Haris away. Haris never saw the ogre smile, his two giant front teeth always hidden from view but recently Haris was sure he had seen the hint of a smile as Ronald chased him away.

'Why do you bother that giant creature?' his mother asked worriedly. 'You are the size of one of his teeth. He could seriously hurt you' his mother said. 'But he lives by himself mama' Haris explained. 'Everyone else is too scared of him. I'm worried if I don't mess with him, he will grow grumpy and old' Haris said and his mother smiled. She had always noticed Haris to mess the most with the woodpeckers who were either old or lonely. While it made her proud to see her son caring for everyone, it terrified her that he wasn't as scared of the ogre as everyone else. With a smell of old socks, a massive body with a tiny head, the ogre was smelly and scary. Before she could lecture him some more, he took off after spotting his friends.

'Hey! Hey!' Haris called out as his friend Jerry and George stopped midflight. 'We're going to the park' they called out, motioning at him to join them. 'I'm going mom' Haris said giving his mother a peck on the cheek and taking off before she could say anything. 'Why are we going to the park?' Haris asked knowing no one went there anymore. Settled high in the canopy of trees was the once new park which now had vegetation growing everywhere. The swings had all been pecked through by the babies and no one had replaced them. The tree had grown even taller, causing half the park to collapse. 'You'll see' his friend Romero said, flapping his tiny wings.

They flew past the houses and turned upwards towards the top of the trees. 'Where are we going?' Haris asked again as his friends continued to go higher and higher. 'You'll see' they repeated annoyed. Reaching the top, Haris panted a little out of breath. 'Look around' his friend instructed. Haris looked around and remembered how much he loved being on top of this tree. It gave a clear view all the way to the river and beyond. At this time, the Sun was high in the sky, causing the river to sparkle and glitter. Other birds whizzed in an out of the trees while Haris spotted other animals swinging from the trees.

'It's beautiful as always' Haris said but his friends shook their heads. 'No! Look there' Ronald said, pointing with one green tipped wing. Haris followed his gaze and saw something he had missed before. The ogre lived towards the upper end of the river but there was activity at the lower end, closer to their village. 'What is that?' Haris asked in wonder as he saw two legged creatures walking around shiny grey things on their shoulders, carrying logs of wood. Scattered around them were fallen trees. 'No one pecks a tree all the way through!' Haris exclaimed in shock. It was the absolute law. No woodpecker was allowed to peck a tree all the way through because it would cause the tree to fall. When a tree fell, it brought down hundreds of homes with it, leaving animals homeless.

'They are called humans' Spence said, shuddering. 'Are they cleaner ogres?' Haris asked looking at their two legs but Spence shook his head. 'They are something else. The legend says wherever they go, destructions follows. They cut trees. Fires start and floods follow' Ronald whispered dramatically. 'I'm sure those are just legends' Haris said itching to take a closer look. He observed as they chopped pieces of wood from the fallen tree. Suddenly the air shuddered, tremors carrying all the way to the canopy top. 'What the-?' Spence said frightfully as birds rose in terror.

Cacaw! Cacaw!

Chirp! Chirp!

Birds and animals yelled out for their loved ones in panic. Eventually the tremors stopped. 'I told you the legends were true' Spence whispered but Haris's eyes were glued miles away. He watched in horror as the human shut off the thing causing tremors and stepped away from the tree. The tree swung a little and Haris prayed it wouldn't fall. 'Oh no! Oh no! Oh no!' he whispered but the tree continued to swing dangerously. It tilted to one side and birds and animals shot out of it. Despite the distance, Haris saw little eggs falling from nests, crashing to the ground while baby birds struggled to fly. The tree continued to tilt until-

CRASHHHHH!

It fell to the ground with a thud that sent another wave through the forest, causing animals and birds to shriek in distress. 'Mom' Haris yelled, flying with all his might trying to find his mother. 'Mom!' he called out as he heard similar shouts of worry around him. Spotting the familiar bright red head with yellow edges, Haris collided with his mother hugging her. 'Mom!' he cried, thick tears falling down his face. 'I saw the most terrifying thing' he hiccupped through the tears, telling her everything he had seen. 'I was so worried' his mother said, hugging him tightly, scared to let her little baby go.

Despite the sun still high, there was a strange silence in the forest air. No one worked, the children stayed at home. Everyone was terrified and sad at what had happened. 'They are talking about the animals moving here' Haris heard his mother talk to his father. As the Sun set and the sounds of destruction went away, the animals and birds got out of their homes. Together the animals marched in a solemn silence while the birds flew in formation, ready to pay tribute to the fallen. Tears fell from every eye as the scenes of destruction came in front of their eyes.

Broken houses were scattered and animals lay injured. The once majestic trees were lying cut on the ground. Reaching the sight, the sick were tended to. The birds carried seeds in their beaks while the animals carried dirt. Together, they replanted the site where the trees had fallen. The hurt animals were carried to safer place as the homeless were consoled.

'We need a plan' Aima, the animal leader spoke. 'We need to get rid of the humans' Cuckooa the bird leader declared. 'We pelt them with rocks and drive them away while you destroy their tree cutters' Cuckooa said and they agreed. 'We attack in the morning' Aima said as everyone got up to prepare.

The next morning the children were strictly told to not leave their homes. The adults packed their pieces of rocks leaving the children to wait. The morning passed in silence as the children waited for new, worried. As the Sun began to sink, the animals and birds returned home defeated. 'We were no match for them. They can hurt us from far distances' Haris's father told his mother sadly. 'What will we do now?' she asked sadly. 'We will have to leave our homes if the animals get here' his father said simply causing his mother to cry even harder.

The air around the forest was full of sorrow. No one wanted to leave their happy town behind. Haris was having dinner with his parents quietly when a sound of heavy footsteps echoed around the forest. 'What's that now?' Haris's mother exclaimed. Leaving their dinner, they left the nest to see the entire neighborhood was out. 'What is it?' Haris's mother asked her neighbor. 'It's-'

she began scared as the footsteps came closer. 'It's the ogre' she screamed as a huge shadow fell over the town.

Birds watched from every corner as a confused Ronald entered, looking around at the birds surrounding him. 'Haris?' he called out in a heavy voice. 'Oh no!' Haris's mother yelled, afraid the ogre was here to take her baby away.

'Haris? Here?' Ronald asked a terrified parrot who simply pointed in Haris's direction, his feather ruffling from fear. 'Ronald?' Haris called out even as his mother tried to hide him.

'Haris? Okay?' The ogre asked and Haris frowned in confusion, flying to the ogre. 'Yeah! I'm fine' Haris said pointing to himself.

'Haris no show. Ronald worried' the ogre said gently lifting one of Haris's feather to check if the baby woodpecker was indeed okay. 'You were waiting for me?' Haris asked surprised and Ronald nodded. 'Ronal like Haris. Haris funny' Ronald growled causing Haris to laugh in delight. 'I knew you liked me' Haris laughed. 'See mom? I told you he liked me' he said to his mother who was still watching in shock. Flying to Ronald's shoulder, Haris settled there. 'I couldn't come because of the humans' Haris explained. Launching in the story of how the humans had cut trees and would cut more until Haris and his family would have to leave, he explained everything to the ogre who listened attentively.

'Haris no leave' Ronald said frowning. 'I don't have a choice' Haris said sadly. A couple of moments passed in silence as the birds went back to their dinner, stunned by this friendship. 'I help chase humans' Ronald finally said. Haris looked at him, sizing him up. 'That could help' he finally said. 'Wait here' he said excitedly as he flew to his father.

'Come here dad! Come here!' Haris pulled his father outside. ' Ronald has an idea' he said excitedly. He listened to what the ogre said and before long an animal meeting was called.

'Hello Ogre sir' Cuckooa said a little unsure as the animals sat in a circle with Ronald sitting among them. 'Ronald save home' he said and everyone nodded. 'We faced defeat because they saw us coming and had time to react. We had no time to surprise them or destroy their tree cutters. Tomorrow we attack again. Ronald will scare them away for good and we will attack their tree cutters' Aima declared.

The next morning dawned and everyone woke excited. They were going to save their homes!

'No more cutting trees! No more cutting trees!'

The animals and birds chanted together as they made their way through the forest, Ronald leading the way. Reaching the edge of the forest, the animals and birds stopped, hiding in the bushes while Ronald got ready to jump.

ROAAAARRRRRRR!

Ronald roared jumping out. The humans screamed in terror as they saw an ogre four times their size.

ROOOOOAAARRRRR!

Ronald roared again. The animals and birds watched happily as the humans dropped whatever they were carrying and ran. Climbing on to their trucks, they drove away faster and faster. Before long, the last human had left. Animals and birds stormed out together, destroying whatever tree cutters were left.

'No more cutting trees! No more cutting trees!' They chanted happily.

Children came out and everyone danced together, happy at keeping their home safe.

Thank you for reading and using this book, you have already taken a step towards your relaxation

Best Wishes

CPSIA information can be obtained
at www.ICGtesting.com
Printed in the USA
BVHW051507080321
601999BV00001BB/78

9 781954 320819